# The Candy Well

Nancy,

Hope you enjoy the book. Thanks for coming.

Sincerely

Bud Wainscott

# The Candy Well

Bud Wainscott

authorHOUSE®

AuthorHouse™
1663 Liberty Drive
Bloomington, IN 47403
www.authorhouse.com
Phone: 1-800-839-8640

Interior Graphics/Art Credit: Regina Puente

Published by AuthorHouse    08/10/2012

ISBN: 978-1-4772-5349-6 (sc)
ISBN: 978-1-4772-5357-1 (e)

Library of Congress Control Number: 2012913475

The book, <u>The Candy Well</u>, is dedicated to the hundreds of students I've encountered in classrooms throughout the country.

It was always my desire to excite and motivate students to use the fantastic creative abilities that each and everyone has within their power. Imagination is a special gift we all have.

The students have ranged in age from primary grades to seniors in high school. Also, I've shared many of my writings with adults, including fellow teachers, administrators and parents.

Hopefully, many will enjoy my writings as much as I have enjoyed creating them.

Sandi lived quite close to her school. That is, if she was able to walk directly to it. There was one big catch. Between her house and her school was a very large wooded area. It was private property. There was a narrow path connecting Sandi's neighborhood with the school property. However, both ends of the path were gated and locked. She had been on the path with her scout troop. Also, her class had taken a nature walk through the woods on a couple of occasions. But she knew better than to be in the woods by herself.

Sandi usually walked to school with her friends. They had to take the sidewalk around the woods. Sometimes she would ride her bike, which saved about ten minutes. It was a twenty minute walk to school. On bad days, Sandi's mother or a neighbor would drive her to school. Sandi always knew she could make it to school in five minutes if she was allowed to go through the woods. But that was never an option for her or anyone else in the neighborhood. Only groups with adults could get permission to be in the woods. They knew that it could be a dangerous area. The light was dim in the woods even in the daytime. The trees were very close together with very little room for the sunlight to shine through. But Sandi always imagined what a fun place the woods would be with her friends.

The wooded area was quite large with its share of animals. Many of the animals were small but could be dangerous with bites from snakes, rats, raccoons, deer and opossums. Also, the brush in the woods was high and thick, if you got off the main path. At night, Sandi would lie in bed listening for animal cries from the woods. Many times, her imagination would run wild thinking about the hidden mysteries of the woods. Little did she realize that she was soon to have the adventure of her life in the woods. It was Friday afternoon and school was about over. Sandi liked Fridays. This Friday was special. On Saturday, she was going to a birthday party at the skating rink. Many of her friends would be at the party.

A real fun weekend was just a few hours ahead. She looked forward to Friday's for other reasons, her class had art and P.E. on Fridays. She really liked the activities in P.E. It was a time to run and jump and yell without getting into trouble. Art was special because she loved to draw and create scenes with flowing colors. Mrs. Craner, Sandi's art teacher, sometimes played music during art class.

Well, the day was just about over and Mrs. Craner asked Sandi if she could stay a few minutes after school to help clean up. She quickly agreed to stay since she had created quite a mess herself. There had been a lot of cutting and many of the scraps had ended up on the floor.

The final bell rang. It was three thirty in the afternoon and time to head home for the weekend.

"Mrs. Craner, I will need to call my mother and tell her that I am staying for a few minutes to help you. I know it will be okay with mom, but she worries if I am late getting home. I walked to school this morning, so I can not stay too late."

"Sandi" Mrs. Craner said, "Please use the phone in the cafeteria. Tell your mother that we should be finished by four thirty and that will give you plenty of time to get home before dark." Sandi hurried down to the cafeteria and called home. "Mom, Mrs. Craner would like for me to stay awhile to help clean up the art room. It is not punishment. She asks different ones to help clean up each Friday. We should be finished by four thirty and I will be home around four forty-five. It should still be light outside."

Sandi's mother was glad to hear her request. She knew the mess Sandi could make when she was really into cutting and designing patters. A lot of the cleaning up was probably of her own doing.

"Yes, Sandi, you may stay for awhile to help Mrs. Craner. I am proud of you and your willingness to help. Art has always been special to you but you must be home at four forty-five we are eating at five. Do not be late, your father has a meeting after dinner."

Sandi rushed back to the art room to help Mrs. Craner. "I have to leave by four thirty."

The time passed quickly and they cleaned the room while talking and listening to music. Mrs. Craner allowed Sandi to choose the music. This was a special treat for her.

Suddenly, Sandi looked at the clock. "Mrs. Craner, it is four forty and I need to hurry home. I cannot be late for dinner and be grounded for the weekend. The big Saturday skating party was on her mind.

"Sandi, I will drive you home, let's go." "No, Mrs. Craner, you live on the other side of town. I can be home by five. It is still light and I will hurry. See you, Monday."

As Sandi turned the corner, she remembered she had forgotten her new jacket. She ran back to school but the door was locked and all the lights were off. Sandi knew Mrs. Craner parked her car behind the school so she ran to the parking lot. She arrived just in time to see Mrs. Craner drive away. Sandi yelled and waved but Mrs. Craner was too far down the street.

Now Sandi was getting very nervous. She ran back to the front of the school. She stood there thinking. She stared at the path that went through the woods directly to her home. She was late and knew she would not make it home in time walking the long way around the woods.

Quickly, Sandi climbed over the gate and started running down the path through the woods. It was still light near the gate because the trees were not too close together near the entrance. Sandi could see the path clearly as she ran faster and faster. The path was about four feet wide and easy to follow, but after a few minutes of running, the path seemed less wide. It was also getting dark. The trees were closer together, letting in less and less light.

Sandi slowed to a walk and started talking to herself. "I know that I am close to home. I should be seeing the lights in my neighborhood. It is really hard to see the path. As long as I stay on the flat, smooth surface I will be okay. Gosh, I can not see anything. It is as dark as night."

Now, Sandi started to panic. She lost the feel of the path and took a sudden right turn into the weeds and grass.

Sandi quickly realized that she was off the path and stopped. Sandi turned around to go back to the path. Her about face returned her to the path but instead of turning right on the path to go home. Sandi walked across the path back into the tall weeds on the other side. Now, she was losing her sense of direction. She looked to the right and then to the left, confused. With every step, she was walking deeper into the woods, instead of toward the path home. She was lost.

As Sandi was stumbling around she suddenly fell into a very large, deep, hole. The hole was so deep, that Sandi could not reach the top. When Sandi realized that she was not hurt, she started looking at the hole.

The hole appeared to be round and about five feet from the bottom to the top. Sandi could touch the sides by stretching out her arms. She could not remember her father or anyone else talking about holes in the woods.

Sandi realized she was now in big trouble. She was late for dinner and had done something she was not supposed to do. She was in a hole with no way of getting out. The skating party on Saturday did not seem too important, right now. The hole was beginning to feel cold and damp. The light was fading and the night was becoming cool and damp.

Sandi was afraid and started to cry, "Help, help, I'm lost and can not get out of this hole or find my way home. I should have stayed on the sidewalk. Can anyone hear me? I need someone to help me. Help, help, help me."

Well, Sandi's voice was heard, not by people, but by the animals in the woods. There were many animals in the woods, some very dangerous. She began to hear the sounds of the forest. Sandi realized that she needed to be quiet or she would attract animals to the hole. Many animals were already at the top looking down at her. She knew she had no way to defend herself if a large raccoon or a wild dog jumped in the hole. Sandi was really upset. She sat down in the bottom of the hole trying to stay quiet. She kept thinking out loud. "Surely, someone will come looking for me. I know my parents have talked to Mrs. Craner. The police have probably been called. Any minute I will hear someone call my name. They will be in the woods, with flashlights, even though I am not supposed to be in here. I wish they would come soon."

As the air became cooler, Sandi buttoned up her blouse and blew on her hands to try to stay warm. She sat down, leaning against the side of the hole and began to nod her head. Before long, she was fast asleep.

"Sandi, wake up. I can help you find your way home. "She opened her eyes and thought she was dreaming and heard a voice offering to help. "Sandi, look up here. I can help you get out and find your way home. "Sandi looked up but could not believe her eyes. There, standing at the top of the hole was a small, stick of candy. It was striped red, white and green. Suddenly, it lit up like a light bulb. Now she could see that the candy stick had a small head, legs and hands. It also had two eyes, a nose, mouth and ears. On top of the head was a small red cap.

"I must be dreaming. Maybe I hit my head when I fell into this hole. You can not be real. You look like a candy stick, but you are talking."

"Sandi, you are not dreaming. I am a candy man and you have fallen into my house, a candy well. "The top is usually covered, but I was out in the woods and left the top off for a few minutes. Usually, we know when people are in the woods and we stay hidden and keep the candy wells covered. The top looks just like the rest of the ground." "Why do you call this dirty hole a candy well? It is just a mud hole that I had the misfortune to fall into." "Sandi, I will help you get out. First, I would like for you to lick your finger and touch the side of the well and then, taste it."

"No way, that wall is just dirt and I am not going to lick dirt. "Finally the candy man convienced Sandi to taste the wall of the well, especially since the candy man would help her out of the hole and find her way home. She rubbed her finger along the side of the wall and slowly licked her finger. "Man, this tastes good. This is the best chocolate candy I have ever tasted. I am going to try all around the wall and the floor.

Wow, I can not believe this. It is not one particular candy, but all of my favorite candies put together. I thought I had fallen into a big dirt hole. This is terrific, Mr. Candyman, may I take some of this well with me? No one will believe this. It may soften my punishment when I get home."

"No, Sandi, you can take nothing with you except your memories. This must remain our secret. No one knows about these candy wells but you. Now, if I show you the way home, will you promise never to tell anyone about this and promise to never come looking for a well, ever again? Sandi, do you know what a promise is?"

"Of course I know what a promise is. It means that I give you my word that I will never tell or show anyone. It will always be our secret."

"Okay, Sandi, I am trusting you to keep your promise. Now, put one foot on one side of the well and one foot on the other side. Just walk up the sides until you reach the top and grab on to a bush. The candy sides are soft and sticky and that will help you climb."

At last, Sandi was out of the hole. Just as the candy man promised, Sandi was led out of the woods by the little candy man, all lit up in red, white and green flashing colors.

They walked down the path to the gate that was just across the street from Sandi's house. She climbed over the gate and turned to thank the candy stick man.

"Sandi, you do not need to thank me, just please remember to keep your promise. Here take this special candy bar with you to remember me. It is very special, but remember, never eat all of it. Always keep a piece for another time. You can share it with your family and friends but do not tell anyone about me or my candy well. You will find the candy bar to be a very unusual piece of candy. It is the most delicious candy you will ever eat."

Suddenly, the candy stick man was gone. Sandi looked at her watch and it was six o'clock. She thought it was much later. She ran up to the front door and prepared herself for the worst.

"Sandi, her mother said, where have you been? We have been so worried. We called Mrs. Craner and she said you left school about four forty. She said she offered to bring you home. I told you we needed to eat dinner at five so that your father would be on time for his six o'clock meeting. Well, we ate dinner without you. There are some leftovers in the refrigerator. I was just about to call the police. Eat your dinner and go straight to your room. You of course are grounded for the weekend."

Sandi's mother was very upset with her. Just before she went to her room, the telephone rang, her friend called to say the birthday party was postponed for a week. So being grounded for the weekend was not as bad as Sandi expected.

Sandi's mother was in no hurry to hear her story until her father came home. Sandi was anxious to taste the candy bar. The wrapping was different from anything you could buy in the store. The foil wrapping was red, white, and green. There was no writing on the wrapper.

Slowly, carefully, she unwrapped the candy. She remembered what the candy man had said and saved some of the candy for later. She decided to rewrap the candy each time in the special foil wrapping. The piece of candy was covered with chocolate and looked just like the other candy that she had eaten before. The first bite was something she would remember for a long time. It was the best tasting candy Sandi had ever eaten. The candy was a mixture of a lot of different candies. It was so good she almost forgot to save a small piece for later. She rewrapped the piece of candy in the special foil wrapper and hid it is a special place.

The next morning after Sandi had gotten dressed she hurried to check the piece of candy that she hidden the night before. She could hardly believe her eyes. The candy bar looked like a brand new one. It was back to the original size. Sandi thought, this is impossible, but there it was, just like she had unwrapped, a whole, new bar of candy.

"Wow, the candy stick man was right. This candy bar is most unusual." As long as the candy bar was not totally eaten, it would go back to its original size.

Sandi was happy to share her candy with family and friends. But she was always careful never to eat all of it. She always saved a piece for later. Everyone always wanted to know where she had bought such terrific candy. She, of course, had not bought the candy from a store. Sandi just told everyone that the candy could not be purchased at a store. It was a gift from a friend. She also, did not say that the candy could grow back to the original size.

Sandi continued to have dreams about the candy well and the candy stick man. She really wanted to see them one more time.

One Saturday morning, Sandi's father was going into the woods to check for trees that had been struck by lightning in a bad storm. She asked if she could go with him to check the trees. She liked the idea of leaving the main path to look for fallen trees. She, however, had another reason for tagging along with her father. She wanted to snoop around for signs of the candy well. She would not mention anything to her father about the well, she was just going to keep her eyes open for any signs of the well.

After about three hours, Sandi's father told her it was time to head home. She trailed a few feet behind, looking for signs of a candy well. She was looking in just about the same spot where she had met the candy stick man.

As she closed the gate to the woods, she heard a soft, familiar voice. She would recognize that voice anywhere. Sandi's father was already across the street and in their house. She was standing by the locked gate, looking back into the woods.

She did not see the candy man."Where are you?" she said."I know I heard you whisper. You can come out, I am by myself." "There was a long silence.

Then the candy stick man appeared close to the gate. He was not lit up and blended in with the woods around him. Sandi could see that the candy man looked very sad and there were tiny tears coming down his cheeks. She then realized what she had done. She had broken her promise. Softly the candy man began to talk."Sandi, I am so sad and disappointed. I really thought I could trust you. You broke your promise. I saw you come into the forest this morning with your father. I saw that your father was inspecting the fallen trees. I was hoping that you were with him to help. Then I realized that you came to look for the candy well and me. You told me that you knew what a promise

33

means. I believed you and I trusted you. What does this mean? Are you determined to find one of our wells?"

Sandi felt really bad. She had promised never to speak of the candy well. She had also promised that she would not look for the candy stick man. She had broken her promise to someone that had probably saved her life. She could hardly speak.

"My little friend, my very special little friend, I am so sorry I broke my promise. I have learned a very important lesson, today. Please, if you will just let me promise one more time. I truly will never come looking for you or the candy well, again. Please, Mr. Candyman, give me one more chance. You are a good friend and I do not want to ruin our friendship, even if we never see each other again. I promise to honor my word this time." Again, there was silence. "Sandi, I will give you one last chance. I believe you deserve a second chance under the circumstances. It is not every day that someone sees a candy stick man or falls into a candy well," The little candy stick appeared happier. He lit up for one brief moment and then he vanished into the woods. Sandi ran across the street into the house. She was feeling good because the candy stick man had given her a second chance.

After dinner, Sandi's family was talking about what they might eat for dessert that night. She had just the thing. She went to her bedroom and got the candy bar. She cut the candy into small pieces and gave some to everyone. Sandi remembered to save a piece for another time. They all said, "This candy is really good." They wanted to know where Sandi had gotten the candy bar. This time she remembered her promise and shared no details of where she had gotten it.

There was a large candy factory in Sandi's town. The factory had been there for a very long time. It made and sold different kinds of candy all over the world. The factory was successful because the candy was so good. Sandi had eaten all of their candy many times. The factory donated candy to her school for prizes and special occasions. But she knew that her candy bar tasted better than anything made at the candy factory in town. In fact, everyone that had tasted the candy begged Sandi to take the candy to the factory to have the owner taste it. Some people thought the candy could be worth a lot of money. She was unsure about taking her candy to the factory owner. She wondered if that would be breaking her promise to the candy stick man. But, she reasoned that the candy stick had told her she could share the candy with everyone. Good candy like this should be shared with everyone. So, she decided to visit the candy factory and speak to Mr. Elliott, the owner of the factory. On Saturday morning Sandi decided she would go see Mr. Elliott. Mr. Elliott was usually at the factory, even though the factory was closed. She did not know if she would be able to see Mr. Elliott because he was a very busy man and she did not have an appointment. Sandi did call for an appointment but was told to just stop by around ten. Mr. Elliott would see her if he was not too busy. So she walked down to the factory with her candy bar in her pocket. Sandi lived near the factory so it did not take her very long to get there. While waiting for Mr. Elliott, she started a conversation with Mr. Elliott's secretary."Mrs. Sandoval, would you like to taste one of the most fantastic candy bars in the whole world? The candy that you make here is really good but the candy I have in my pocket is better that any candy made anywhere in the world. Here, take a piece." She cut a small piece and handed it to Mrs. Sandoval."Young lady, you are already a super salesman, even at your young age. But I will be hard to convince after working so many years at the candy factory. I have been around the best, tasted them all. What kind of candy have you handed me, Sandi? Who makes it?" Sandi handed Mrs. Sandoval the wrapped candy bar."Sandi, this is really strange. The foil wrapper is pretty, but there are no words on it. Every candy wrapper has printed information on it. Is this generic candy? Are you sure it is safe to eat? I am a littler confused about the candy." "Mrs. Sandoval, the candy is safe. I have shared it with my family, friends, teachers and pastor. No one has gotten sick from eating the candy. In fact, they all agree that it is the best candy they have ever tasted. Go ahead, try it and tell me what you think about the candy." Finally, Mrs. Sandoval put the piece of candy into her mouth.

Sandi wished she had a camera with her to capture the expression on Mrs. Sandoval's face. She could not believe the fantastic taste. "This is the best candy I have ever tasted" Mrs. Sandoval said. The words were out of her mouth shortly after swallowing the first bite. "Oh, don't tell Mr. Elliott I said that. He definitely needs to see you. I will just call to see if he is ready to see you." Mrs. Sandoval picked up the phone and dialed Mr. Elliott's office. "Mr. Elliott, Sandi is here to see you. Remember we told her to stop by on Saturday morning. Sir, you can not be too busy to give Sandi just a few minutes of your time. I know you will be pleased with what this young lady has to share with you. Yes, I realize you are busy. Alright, I will send her right in. Sandi, Mr. Elliott will see you now. He is very busy but will give you a few minutes of his time. Please, let me know how your meeting comes out."

Sandi slowly walked to Mr. Elliott's door. She gently knocked on the door. Sandi had only seen Mr. Elliot once at her school when she was in the first grade. She remembered he had a loud, rough voice and was very tall. Suddenly, the door opened. "Young lady, please come in. I understand you have something to share with me. May I offer you some candy? I know you have probably tasted most of it." "Yes, sir, I have tasted your candies before. They are really good. But I do not need any right now, thank you. I would really like to share with you some candy that I have. With all due respect, it is better than any candy that is made here, and yours is great." Sandi held out the candy bar for Mr. Elliott to look at and hopefully taste. Mr. Elliott took the candy bar. He studied the wrapping very carefully. "Sandi, where did you get this? The wrapper has no words on it. It tells nothing about the candy. Candy can not be sold like this. Where did you buy it? You must tell me. Stores are not allowed to sell candy packaged like this."

"Sir, I did not buy it. A special friend gave it to me several weeks ago. Maybe he made it, I am not really sure. I did not ask him anything about it. The candy is not only great tasting, but it regenerates itself. I just wrap up what is left at the end of the day and the next day I have a whole new candy bar."

Mr. Elliott could not help but laugh as he listened to Sandi tell him about her unusual candy. He was fascinated with her imagination. He finally unwrapped the candy bar. One piece was missing. "I thought you said the candy regenerated itself. What happened to the missing piece?" Sandi replied, "I gave a piece to your secretary, Mrs. Sandoval. And, yes, the candy bar does grow back over night."

Mr. Elliott bit into the candy. Immediately he realized this was no ordinary candy. The candy had a special flavor and texture. He quickly took a second and third bite. Of, course, Sandi did not let him eat all of it. "Sandi, this is better than anything we make. I believe we could make this candy right here in the factory. The scientist in my laboratory could break the candy down and determine what the ingredients are. Then we would know how to reproduce it in great quantities. Sandi, may I keep the candy bar over night to see what it looks like tomorrow? I would like for you to come back tomorrow at two. Then we will unwrap it together." Sandi agreed to leave the candy with Mr. Elliott until the next day.

Before leaving, she reminded Mr. Elliott not to eat all of the candy. Mr. Elliott agreed to leave the candy wrapped until the next day. Sandi said goodbye and left the office. As she left the factory, she mentioned to Mrs. Sandoval that Mr. Elliott liked the candy and that she would return tomorrow.

That night Sandi had trouble sleeping, she kept having dreams. She was worried about the candy bar and what she would do with it. What would the candy stick man want her to do. It was a long night for her.

Morning finally came and it was time for Sandi to go back to the candy factory. She was worried about the candy bar. She wondered if her candy bar would still be there. Had it regenerated itself for Mr. Elliott? Had Mr. Elliott eaten it all? Thoughts were swirling through her head. Did the candy stick man know what she had done and if he did, what would he think?

Mrs. Sandoval was happy to see Sandi. She told her that Mr. Elliott was waiting to see her. Mr. Elliott greeted her with a handshake.

"Sandi, we just couldn't wait. We have examined your candy bar very carefully. My scientists have broken it down to its finest point. They think they know exactly how to reproduce it. And yes, it did regenerate itself over night. We have no clues as to how that happened. We will probably never know. Sandi, I have an offer for you. I would like to buy your candy bar. I know you would like to share this special taste with people all over the world. We can make the candy bar by the thousands. I am offering you one hundred thousand dollars, new bicycles for you and your family, a new car, and all the candy you and your family can eat for the rest of your life. I have spoken to your parents about the offer. They were shocked that one candy bar could be worth so much money. But they said the decision was yours. We would put the money in the bank, in a trust for you and buy everything else immediately. Of course, you and your family may choose the bicycles and car. What do you say, Sandi?"

"Mr. Elliott, are we allowed to do this? Could you get in trouble by making and selling someone else's candy? After all, we do not know too much about the history of the candy bar."

"Sandi, you told me that someone gave you the candy. He did not tell you what you could or could not do with it. And besides, it has no labels or identification marks. There is no patent registration with the United States government. Yes, we are allowed to reproduce this at our factory. It will be given a name and officially registered with the government. Everything will be legal. We know that we can not make the candy regenerate itself. But the candy does not need that quality. We will be making thousands of the candy bars, even millions. Are you ready to make a deal, Sandi? My factory is ready to start production of the candy next week."

"Okay, let's do it." Sandi said. "When can we pick out the bicycles and car? "With a handshake and the signing of some papers, the deal was done. Sandi and her family got new bicycle and Sandi's mom and dad picked out not one but two new cars. The money was deposited in the bank for Sandi's college education. Everyone was happy.

The next few months were routine. The factory was making thousands of the candy bars and shipping them to all parts of the world. The factory stopped making other kinds of candy. New machinery was set up to make the new candy bar. Millions of dollars were spent on advertising the new candy. As time passed, Sandi thought it was strange that she had heard nothing from the factory. Mr. Elliott said he would send free candy every month but she had received none.

One day, several months later Sandi was shocked to see on the front page of the town newspaper, the headline stating: CANDY FACTORY CLOSING-NEW CANDY BAR COMPLETE FAILURE. Everyone in the town was stunned. The candy factory had been in existence for many years. How could such a thing have happened? Yes, they had taken a big chance with the new candy bar, but everyone who tasted the candy bar thought it was terrific. In fact, they all agreed it was the best candy they had ever tasted. There is no way such a candy bar could fail on the market. Mr. Elliott had experts that had reproduced the candy. The picture in the newspaper showed the parking lot totally empty. The gates to the factory were chained and locked.

Sandi was very sad by the closing. She wanted to talk to Mr. Elliott, to find out what happened. Finally, one Saturday morning she saw Mr. Elliott's car parked at the factory. She decided to wait until Mr. Elliott came out to his car. Around noon, Sandi spotted Mr. Elliott walking to his car. "Mr. Elliott, Mr. Elliott, it's me, Sandi. I was so sorry to hear about the factory closing. Would you tell me what happened? There is no way that candy could fail. I just can not believe it. Please tell me the story. Do I need to give you the money back? What about the cars and bicycles? My family is concerned about the deal we made."

Mr. Elliott stopped, looked over at Sandi and then walked to the fence. "Sandi, this is a very sad time for the factory. What was a very busy candy factory is now a silent building of shut-off machines. We were all convinced that we could duplicate the special candy bar that you brought to us. We thought we knew exactly the ingredients in the candy. But, I guess we really did not know as much as we thought. Thousands of candy bars were produced and shipped to all parts of the world. All of our factory machinery was set up to produce just one kind of candy, the Striped Special. Many of the candy bars were returned to us. I guess the rest were thrown away. They did not sell anywhere. No, Sandi, you do not need to return anything. A deal is a deal. What you sold us was fantastic. What we produced was terrible. When we tested the candy before shipping, it was great. After being wrapped and shipped, it changed. I have a box in my car I'll get it for you. The whole box is yours to keep or throw away." Mr. Elliott handed the box of candy to her.

She quickly opened the box. The candy bars looked the same as the one she had sold to Mr. Elliott. The foil wrapper looked exactly the same and the colors were the same. She could not see any difference in the package. Then, she took a big bite of the candy. Mr. Elliott watched as Sandi bit into the candy. "Yuck! This is terrible candy. This is not what I gave you. It looks the same, it feels the same, but the taste is terrible.

This is the worst candy bar I have ever tasted. What happened? No one would want to buy this candy. Couldn't your experts fix the candy so that it would be good to eat?"

"We tried very hard and spent a great deal of money trying to find what went wrong" Mr. Elliott said. "Sandi, who ever made this candy did not want it to be reproduced. I just wonder where it came from. I guess we will never know the answer to that question. Sandi, take the box of candy home and share it with your family and friends or throw it away. Well, I need to start for home. We all thought we had a winner. Good bye, Sandi."

Sandi hurried home and told her family what Mr. Elliott had told her. Everyone threw the candy away after just one bite. They were all puzzled about the candy. Before long everyone forgot about the candy except Sandi. She wondered if the candy stick man had anything to do with the bad taste of the candy bar. On, Saturdays, Sandi would hang on the gate staring into the woods. She wanted to see the candy stick man just one more time. She just knew the candy stick man would give her some answers.

The days were getting colder. Winter was approaching. The beautiful season of Fall was just about over. It was late October and most of the leaves were on the ground. The woods were beginning to look very bare. Soon, snow would be coming down. On the last Saturday morning in October, Sandi was outside playing around the gate by herself. Suddenly, she heard a slight noise near the gate, like an animal or something in the grass. As she looked to see where the sound was coming from, the little candy stickman appeared near the gate post. "Hi, Sandi, I was not going to see you again, but my plans changed. We are leaving the forest. Too many trees are coming down for a new housing development. It will not be safe for us to stay. People will begin to find our holes soon. But, we will be gone. They will wonder about the holes

47

but only you will know the truth. Please, do not tell anyone about us. They probably would not believe you anyway. Sandi, you kept your promise this time. I am so proud of you. Even though you will not know it, I will keep track of you. I wish you the very best. After all, I am a part of your future. I had something to do with it."

"Wait, Mr. Candyman. I have a couple of questions for you. Are you angry with me for selling the candy? And why couldn't they reproduce it? I know you have the answers."

"Sandi, I told you the candy was yours. What you did with it would be your decision. But it was only meant to be special for you. The candy could never be reproduced. That is why I told you to always save a piece for the future. No, I am not angry with you. I do feel badly for Mr. Elliott. The candy bar helped you and that is why I gave it to you. Sandi, I must go. Please remember me and I will remember you. "Suddenly the candy stick man was gone. His light was out.

As Sandi walked back across the street to her house, she felt something hit her on the back of her head. "What was that? "She looked down at the street and saw a very familiar sight. It was wrapped in red, white and green foil. She picked it up, unwrapped it and yes, it was another candy bar. Inside the wrapper was a small note that read, "This bar is yours forever my special parting gift to you."

Sandi never saw the candy stick man again. Yes, some of the holes were found but no signs of candy were found in them. The holes were a mystery to many, but not to Sandi. "I eat my candy and think about my experiences with the candy stick man and his candywell. I still have my old candy wrapper framed and hanging on my wall. The trees are gone but I'll always remember the candy well."


THE END

CPSIA information can be obtained at www.ICGtesting.com
Printed in the USA
LVOW080058150912

298895LV00003B/18/P